CREATE YOUR OWN
SUPERHERO EPIC

FOR FIONA,
MY SUPERHERO

FOR GEORGE

Scholastic Children's Books
An imprint of Scholastic Ltd
Euston House, 24 Eversholt Street, London, NW1 1DB, UK
Registered office: Westfield Road, Southam, Warwickshire, CV47 0RA
SCHOLASTIC and associated logos are trademarks and/or
registered trademarks of Scholastic Inc.

First published in the UK by Scholastic Ltd, 2017

Text and illustrations copyright © Andrew Judge and Chris Judge, 2017

The right of Andrew Judge and Chris Judge to be identified as the authors
of this work has been asserted by them.

ISBN 978 1407 17126 5

A CIP catalogue record for this book
is available from the British Library.

Printed by CPI Group (UK) Ltd, Croydon, CR0 4YY
Papers used by Scholastic Children's Books are made
from wood grown in sustainable forests.

1 3 5 7 9 10 8 6 4 2

www.scholastic.co.uk

CREATE YOUR OWN
SUPERHERO EPIC

ANDREW JUDGE & CHRIS JUDGE

SCHOLASTIC

IMAGINE

if you were a **SUPERHERO!**

Imagine if you were so powerful you could change the world with one hand!

Imagine if you could fold space and rip a hole in time!

Well, **IMAGINE** no more!

Your time has come!

So grab your **STAFF OF INFINITE POWER** (pencil), your **NULLIFICATION DEVICE** (eraser), your **SPECTRUM SUFFUSERS** (crayons) and prepare to save the world!

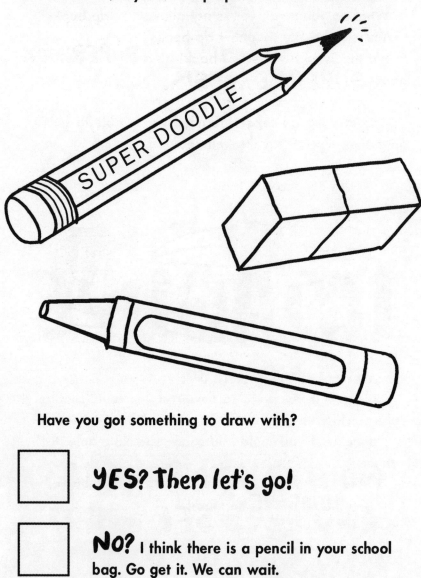

Have you got something to draw with?

☐ **YES?** Then let's go!

☐ **NO?** I think there is a pencil in your school bag. Go get it. We can wait.

We're going to need your help to DRAW, FOLD and RIP our way through this book.

What do you mean you're not allowed to rip books? You're right! You shouldn't rip books.
But this is no ORDINARY book! It's a SUPERBOOK about SUPERHEROES!

And every good superhero needs to be able to RIP open their shirt to reveal their secret identity.

NOW FLY TO PAGE 133 AND LET'S SEE WHAT YOU CAN DO!

That's why they need your **HELP**. So grab a pen or a pencil and finish the Doodles on this page.

Great work! We're nearly ready to start.

One final thing: are you **BRAVE?** Are you willing to battle **GIGANTIC MONSTERS?**

Are you willing to scribble on the faces of evil **SUPERVILLAINS?**

You are? **FANTASTIC!**

I hope you weren't too scared by those **EVIL BAD GUYS,** because some of the villains in this story are even **WORSE!**

I know! It's hard to believe, but it's true. Wait until you meet Unpleasant Desmond. I won't tell you what his superpower is yet, but it is **DISGUSTING!**

Are you sure you want to continue? Are you ready for some **SUPERHERO** action?

☐   **YES.** Let's turn the page to start!

☐   **NO,** I'm too scared. Then go to page 136.

CHAPTER ONE

MAYBE!

In the centre of Doodletown stands a tall tower, the headquarters of **MAYBE INDUSTRIES**.

Not only is it the tallest tower, it's also the coolest. It's got two helicopter pads and a big flag.

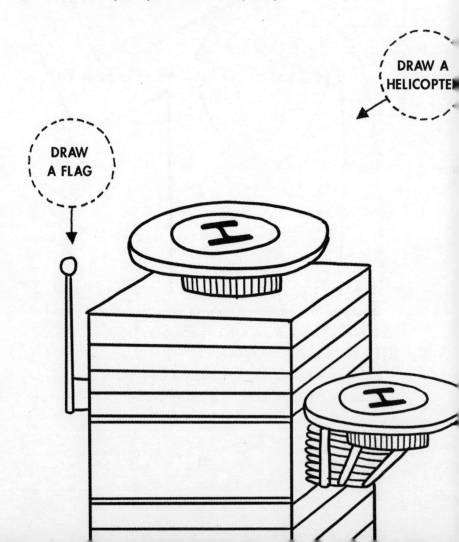

DRAW A
HELICOPTE

DRAW
A FLAG

This is David Maybe, head of Maybe Industries.

David is one of Doodletown's smartest people, and his brilliant inventions have made him very rich. Like, **BILLIONAIRE** rich!

But David hasn't always been a billionaire. In fact, he used to be just the **SON** of a billionaire.

His father, Jess Noah Maybe, invented crayons. Before JN Maybe, Doodletown was a drab, black-and-white town. Crayons changed everything, making Doodletown a wonderfully colourful place to live.

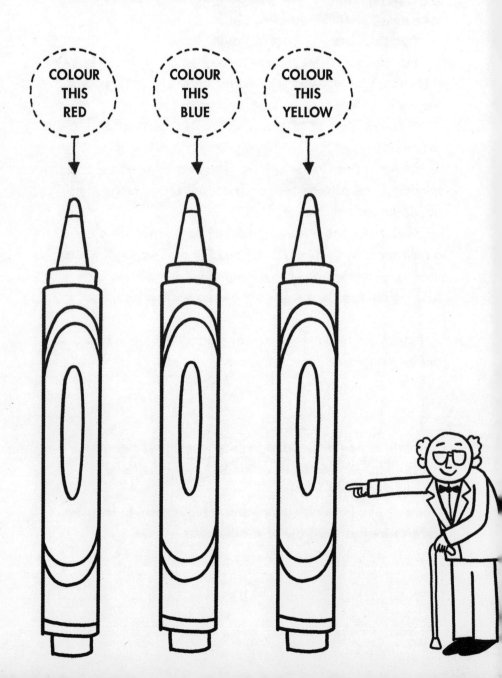

David was very proud of his dad, but he wanted to help Doodles in a different way: he wanted to be a doctor and work in a hospital.

But his dad said, "No son of mine is going to be a DOCTOR! You are going to do something useful and take over the family business."

"But, Dad, what if..." said David.

"No 'what ifs' and 'buts', Maybe," said his dad. "You're a Maybe, and we Maybes always know EXACTLY what we want. I want YOU to take over from me."

So David went to college and worked hard, and eventually got a PhD, which made him a different sort of doctor: a Doctor of Inventions. He returned home and became head of Maybe Industries. But he never gave up his dream of helping people.

Working in the Maybe Industries lab, David developed a new form of UNLIMITED POWER: the Maybe Knot, an energy source powered by quantum entanglement*. He saw right away that it could be used to help people.

By day he is just your average handsome, billionaire, genius inventor...

*Ask your teacher to explain quantum entanglement on Monday.

... but by night he becomes Doodletown's greatest **SUPERHEROES**.

Yes, you read that right! **SUPERHEROES**, plural! David Maybe is so rich, and the Maybe Knot is so powerful, that he has a different alter-ego for every supervillain he has to face.

For example, when seaside scoundrels TuNasty and Smackerel are causing trouble, it's Nori Man who reels them in.

DRAW A HOOK

If he has to battle Fly Guy, the really **ANNOYING** villain who just buzzes around town irritating everyone, he becomes world-famous web slinger www.Man.

DRAW SOME WEB

13

And sometimes he even goes out late at night to fight crime. And I mean **LATE!** Like, 11.30 p.m.!

Crazy, I know! He should be in bed!

But crime never sleeps. And it doesn't stop dancing, either. So Doc Maybe becomes Dirk Knight, the disco-loving caped crusader.

COLOUR THE LIGHTS

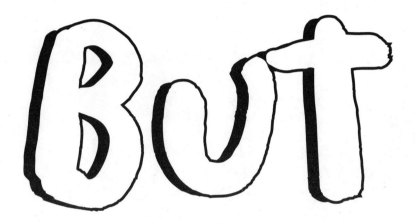

this book is not, in fact, about Doc Maybe.
  It's about what happens when he disappears one day...

Meet Hiro Itazuragaki. Hiro has just won the
Doodletown Doodling Contest by doodling a poodle
eating noodles.

Hiro's prize is a **BIG MEDAL** and the chance to
meet his hero, Doc Maybe.

DRAW
HIRO'S
MEDAL

So here he is, just arriving in Maybe Towers.

"Hello," says Frank the Security Guard. "You must be Hiro. Doc Maybe is expecting you. You had better hurry, though. He is due to make his guest appearance at Hero Con* this afternoon. You can use his private lift. Just press the red button."

"Um," says Hiro, somewhat confused, "which one is red?"

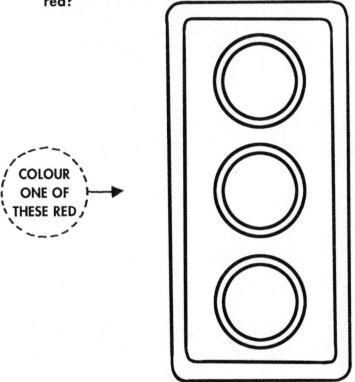

Once the lift arrives you can turn the page.

I hope it arrives soon. Otherwise this book will get really boring.

*See page 135.

CHAPTER TWO

MESS!

When Hiro arrives in the office, it's **EMPTY!** There is no sign of David Maybe.
It looks like there's been **TROUBLE!**

But look, there are some CLUES!

Do you want to check out the broken cage? Then go to page 20.

Or maybe you want to see what's on the computer? Jump to page 36.

Have a look at the footprints? Turn to page 28.

LAB

D. MAYBE, CEO

Hiro kneels down to look at the broken cage.

"Hmm," says Hiro to himself, "I wonder what was in this cage?"

Have you any ideas?

☐ **YES**, it could be a _____ .

☐ **NO**, I'm not really paying attention.

D. MAYB

Suddenly Hiro spots something on the ground, beside the cage.

It is a plastic key card.

Guess where this card is for?
Did you say "Lab"?

 **YES?**

Well done, you! You must be quite smart.

Did you spot the door with "Lab" written above it on page 19?

NO? *

OK, maybe you're not so smart after all...

Hiro checks out the door. It looks like it's a lift. There is a card reader in the wall beside the door.

*What do you mean there is no "Yes" box to check? Who's in charge here?

Hiro slots the key card into the slot. A panel slides open to reveal **MORE** security.

Whatever you did there seems to have worked! The doors slide open and...

...Hiro is attacked by a **MOUSE!**
It is floating in a bubble without any visible means of support. It's a wireless mouse.

"Aargh!" says Hiro, trying to bat away the floating mouse. "I don't like bubble and squeak!"

How is he going to burst the bubbles? He needs
something sharp. Have you any suggestions?

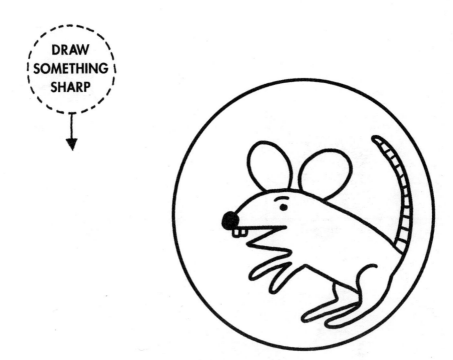

Hiro pokes at the bubble, but nothing works. It won't
POP!

He only succeeds in pushing it towards an open
window.

The mouse floats away.

How strange, thinks Hiro. *Bubbles that can't be burst.
I'd better take some notes.*

Why don't you help Hiro make some notes in his
SuPER IDEAS notebook?

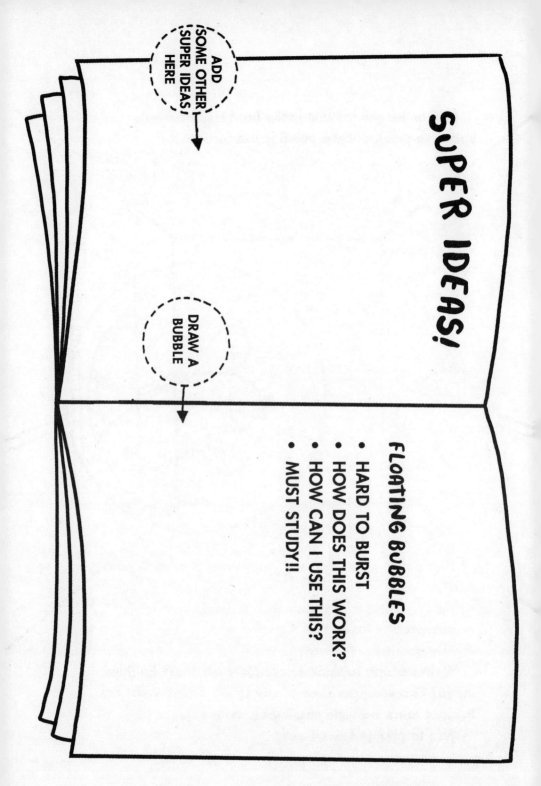

SUPER IDEAS!

ADD
(SOME OTHER
SUPER IDEAS)
HERE

DRAW A
BUBBLE

FLOATING BUBBLES

- HARD TO BURST
- HOW DOES THIS WORK?
- HOW CAN I USE THIS?
- MUST STUDY!!

Hiro enters the lift and looks for a button to press. But the panel is blank.

DRAW BUTTONS

Hiro presses the button for Level 4.

He has plenty to think about. How are these bubbles made? Can you figure out a way to use them? What has this got to do with the missing billionaire?

Turn to page 44.

Hiro follows the footprints across the room. They stop, mysteriously, at a blank wall. He studies the wall closely, but can't see anything that looks like a door.

Hmm, thinks Hiro, *there must be a secret panel?*

Suddenly he notices a tiny switch. He presses it, and a SECRET DOOR opens!

PRESS HERE →

DRAW A DOOR

The door opens into pitch blackness. Hiro peers cautiously inside. He notices that the floor seems to descend downwards into the dark.

"It looks like a slide." Hiro's voice echoes in the void.

He sits down and cautiously pushes off...

WHEEEEE!

Hiro lands with a bump on the floor of a large cave. Hundreds of stalactites hang from the ceiling. Or at least there will be hundreds when you draw more of them.

DRAW
STALACTITES

Hiro suddenly realizes he is in Doc Maybe's World-Famous Secret Underground Lair!
Look, it's Doc Maybe's collection of superhero costumes!

This is **COOL!** It's Doc Maybe's **NORI MAN** costume!
And there's the Cabinet of Super Weapons!

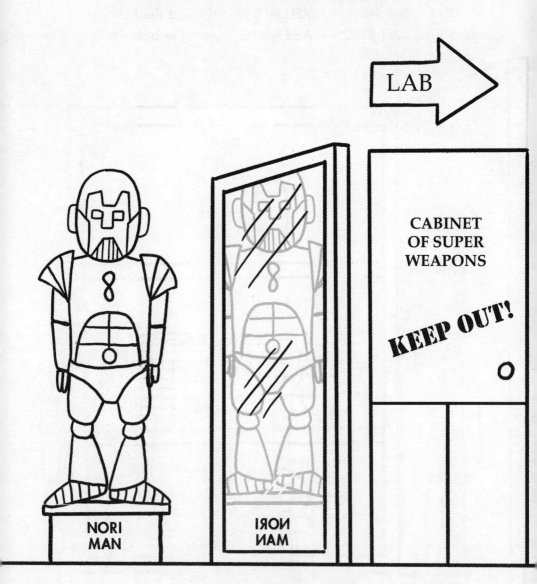

LAB

CABINET
OF SUPER
WEAPONS

KEEP OUT!

NORI
MAN

NORI
MAN

Hiro can't help himself. Despite the warning to **KEEP OUT**, he cautiously opens The Cabinet of Super Weapons and peeps inside.

There's Doc Maybe's **SMELLMET HELMET** and the famous **10-S RACQUET ROCKET**. And what's this on the bottom shelf?

Hiro carefully picks up the dangerous-looking weapon. He carefully points it away from himself and pulls the trigger...

My goodness! It's Doc Maybe's **HAIRDRYER**! No wonder his hair always looks so stylish.

Hiro searches the rest of the lab, but there's still no sign of Doc. Hiro decides to check out the door at the back of the cave. He takes the hairdryer with him. Well, you never know when he might need to dry his hair in an emergency.

There doesn't seem to be a door handle.
Can you draw one for him?

Now turn to page 44.

Hiro checks out the big desk in the middle of the room.

D. MAYBE, CEO

Hiro wants to go through the laptop computer, but he feels a little bit GUILTY doing it without permission.

But hey, Doc Maybe is missing and there might be some clues on it. So I suppose that makes taking a quick peek all right...

But he needs a password to access the computer. Hiro thinks for a moment then types in:

ENTER PASSWORD	123456

Nope, that doesn't work.
Next he tries:

ENTER PASSWORD	PASSWORD

but that doesn't work either.
Can you think of a password? Write it in here:

ENTER PASSWORD	

IT WORKED! How did you guess? The laptop blinks to life.

Hiro stares at the screen. "Wow! What an AWESOME background picture!"

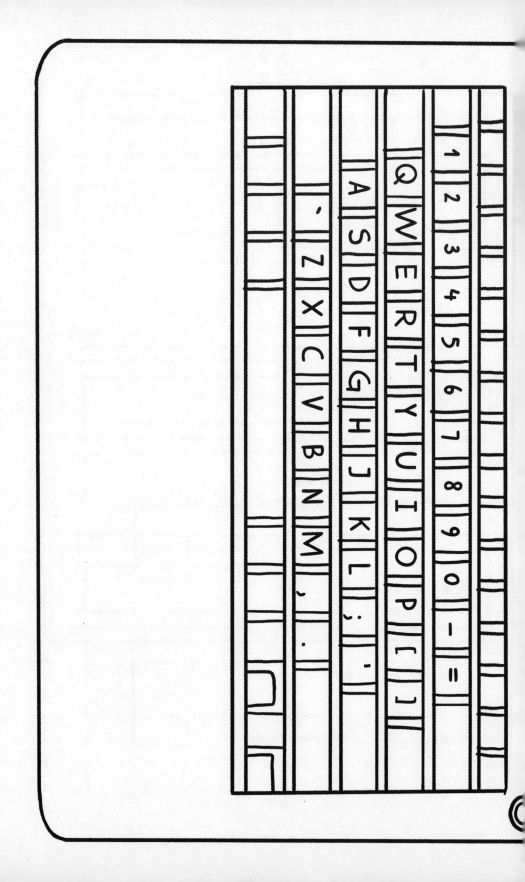

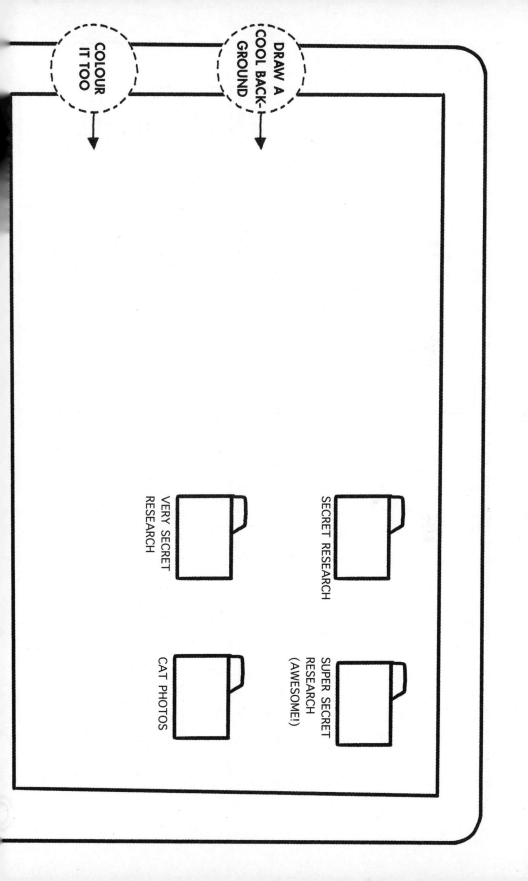

Hiro clicks on the **SUPER SECRET RESEARCH** folder to open it.

Yes, I know you really want to look in the **CAT PHOTOS** folder, but we don't have time for that now. We've an exciting story to get on with!

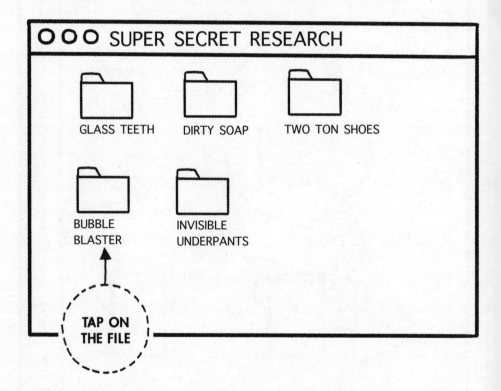

Some of these projects look interesting, thinks Hiro. *Others, not so much.*

The Bubble Blaster file looks the most promising, so he taps on the file and it pops open.

A schematic plan fills the screen.

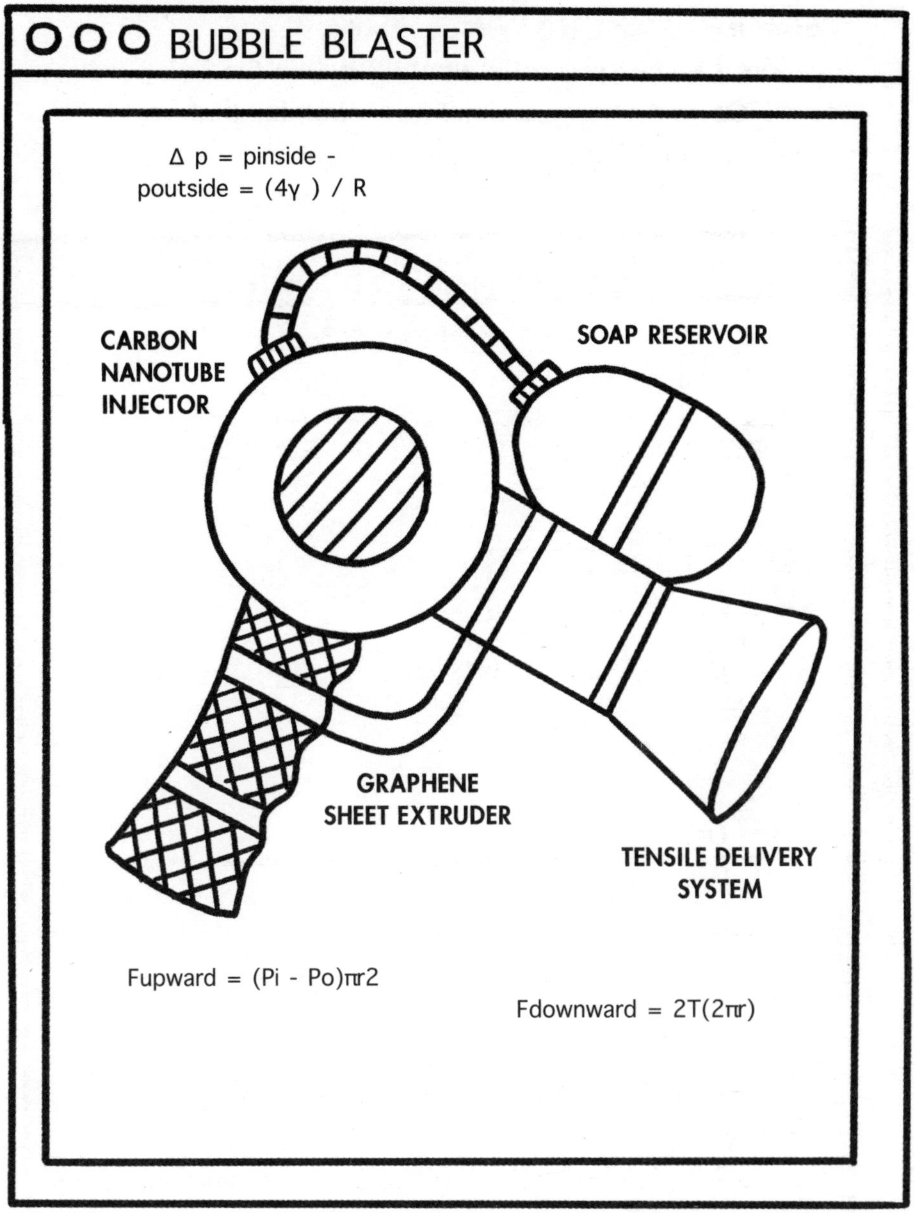

○ ○ ○ BUBBLE BLASTER

Δ p = pinside - poutside = $(4\gamma) / R$

CARBON
NANOTUBE
INJECTOR

SOAP RESERVOIR

GRAPHENE
SHEET EXTRUDER

TENSILE DELIVERY
SYSTEM

Fupward = $(Pi - Po)\pi r2$

Fdownward = $2T(2\pi r)$

Have you any idea what this is?

Well, Hiro is very impressed. "Wow! A bubble machine that blows **UNBURSTABLE** bubbles!"

Imagine what you could do with that!

No, seriously, imagine. Because I can't think of anything...

Write down your ideas here:

CLEVER THINGS TO DO WITH
UNBURSTABLE BUBBLES

1.

2.

3.

4.

5.

Hiro prints out the schematic and sits back in the big chair.

"I wonder where Doc Maybe does all this research?" he says aloud. "Also, I wonder what this big red button under the desk labelled $'LAB'$ is for?"

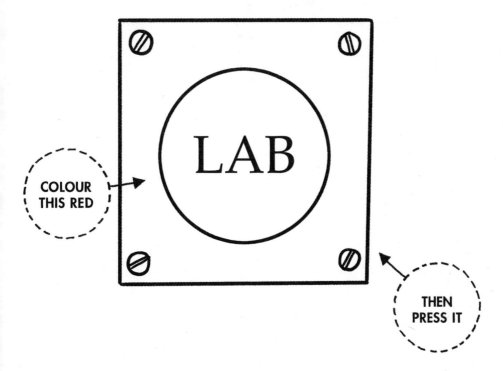

As soon as you press the button, a hatch opens and the chair begins to slowly descend beneath the floor.

"CO

O

L!"

says

Hiro.

CHAPTER TWO

LAB!

Hiro arrives in Doc Maybe's research lab. "Hello?" he calls loudly. There is no reply.

CONNECT THE WIRES

It looks like there is an experiment in progress, but some of the equipment is disconnected. Can you help Hiro fix the experiment?

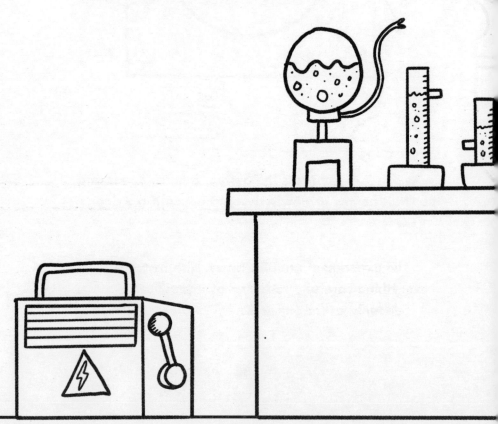

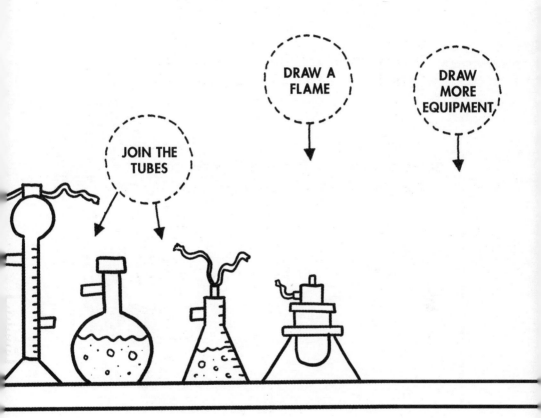

The experiment bubbles away. Hiro watches
everything carefully to see what it produces.
Suddenly, at the far end...

...a big bubble begins forming. It grows larger and larger before breaking free.

Hiro reaches out to pop it. But no matter how hard he pokes it, it won't burst.

Try it yourself. Poke it with your finger. See? It won't burst.

Hiro has a great idea! He searches the lab and
gathers together the various bits and pieces he needs.
Why don't you try drawing all the
pieces together?

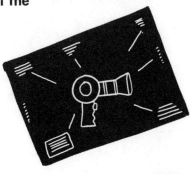

Hiro admires his (and your) handiwork. Time to test it!
He carefully aims the Blaster and pulls the trigger.
It whirrs to life and

DRAW A
BUBBLE

A big floating bubble pops out!

He aims it at the rubbish bin and pulls the trigger. A big bubble expands from the blaster and engulfs the bin, which lifts off and floats to the ceiling.

"Wow!" says Hiro aloud.

He tries again, but something is wrong. Nothing comes out this time. Hiro gives it a shake and pokes the nozzle with his finger.

Suddenly a bubble expands around his hand! He is lifted off the floor and **FLOATS** around the room!

Hiro bumps off the ceiling and hangs there. How is he going to get down?

He pokes the bubble with his finger. Nothing happens.

He tries biting it and pinching it. Nada.

Nothing seems to work. Nothing Hiro does, that is.

But maybe **YOU** can help! Try **POKING** a hole in the page with your pencil!

POKE A HOLE

POP!

Great! That worked! The bubble bursts and Hiro drops to the floor with an "OOF!"

"Thanks," says Hiro. "At least WE know how to burst these bubbles now."

Hiro sits on the floor with his legs out in front of him.

This Bubble Blaster would make a **GREAT** piece of equipment for a new superhero, don't you think?

Hiro thinks so too. "I could use the Bubble Blaster to become a **SUPERHERO** myself! If Doc Maybe is in trouble I could use it to help him. But first, I need a costume."

Well, that shouldn't be a problem. This is the lair of a superhero, after all, and there is a big chest at the back of the lab labelled "**DRESSING UP BOX**".

DRAW CAPE

☐ MASK

☐ CAPE

☐ CIRCLE SHIRT

☐ GLOVES

DRESSING UP BOX

☐ SKULL SHIRT

☐ SHORTS

☐ MASK

☐ HEART SHIRT

☐ WIG

What would you pick if you were choosing a superhero costume? Tick the boxes.

At last, Hiro is nearly ready to be a **HIRO-IC!**
Doesn't he look **SMART**. All it needs now is some
colour. Can you help?

EXCELLENT! Now we're ready for ACTION!

Hiro decides to leave Doc Maybe's lab through the secret **EXIT** door. He takes the secret **LIFT** down to the bottom level. He crawls through the secret TUNNEL.

DRAW HIRO AND HIS ROUTE

He pops out of the secret **EXIT** in front of the
Doodletown Town Hall, just as Mayor Squarehair is
starting his press conference.

"It is with great **ALARM** that I have to confirm the
disappearance of Doodletown's superhero protector Doc
Maybe," the mayor is saying to the reporters.

"I have announced a state of emergency," says the mayor. "Extra police officers will be patrolling the streets. Doodletown is under curfew until Doc Maybe returns. Everyone has to be in bed by 8 p.m.*"

* Curfew sounds a bit like bedtime, doesn't it?

"Excuse me," says Hiro. "Before you overreact, have you thought about **LOOKING** for Doc Maybe? He may be in trouble and need our help."

"And who are you?" asks Mayor Squarehair.

"I'm Hiro Itazuragaki."

"Well, Mr Itazuragaki, I am the mayor," says Mayor Squarehair. "And I say we **PANIC** because that's what people in charge like to do! You go back to playing with your superhero friends at Hero Con, OK?"

And with that the mayor marches off to pass some new laws.

Hero Con, thinks Hiro, *now there's an idea!*

CHAPTER FOUR

HERO CON!

The mayor is right, of course. Doc Maybe is due to make his appearance at Hero Con this afternoon. Did you spot that advert for Hero Con on page 135 earlier?

☐ **YES**

Then write down the location and time here:

LOCATION: _____

TIME: _____

☐ **NO**

Then you had better go to page 135 and have a look! Come back when you are ready.

Hiro arrives at the place you wrote down on the last page. (Well, I'm not going to tell you if YOU don't know already.)

There is a big, bulky doorman blocking his way. He is holding a clipboard. He asks Hiro if his name is on the list.

"I'm not sure," says Hiro.

"If your name is not on the list," the doorman says, "you're not coming in."

INVITED GUEST LIST

DOC MAYBE
MOUSE MASTER
MINI-HEAD
SOCK-EATER LAD
JOIN-THE-DOTS DOTTY
PENCILLER
GELATO LAD
NAUTI-GAL
INKER
KASHIER KID

"Look, a spider," says Hiro, pointing at the opposite page.

The doorman glances around nervously.

QUICK! Add Hiro's name to the list while he's not looking.

The doorman looks back down at his list.
"Oh," he says, "your name IS on the list. In you go, sir."
Hiro smiles and steps through the door into ...

DOODLETOWN'S HERO CONVENTION

This place is GREAT, thinks Hiro. I'll definitely find some SUPERHEROES to help me here.

"Hi," says a hero wearing a giant **PENCIL** costume. "Are you here for the Superhero Symposium or the Costumed Player Contest?"

"I'm not sure," says Hiro.

"Well, do you have a superpower," asks Penciller, "or do you just like dressing up, like I do?"

What do you think Hiro will say?

☐ **YES**, I have a **COOL** super power.

☐ **YES**, I just **LOVE** awesome costumes.

"I can do **THIS!**" says Hiro, holding up the Bubble Blaster.

"Blow-drying your hair isn't really a superpower," says Penciller.

"No," says Hiro. "It's not a hairdryer. Watch!"

Penciller is impressed. "Wow! Unburstable bubbles! I am **IMPRESSED**."

By now, a crowd has gathered. They are whooping and cheering as Hiro continues his bubble show.

"Make this ice-cream float," shouts Gelato Lad.

"Float my boat," says Nauti-Gal.

"I need to see my cash float," says Kashier Kid.

Hiro continues to fire bubbles into the air. A motley collection of heroes has gathered around him, including Penciller.

DRAW BUBBLES AROUND THESE

Penciller claps Hiro on the back and gives him a big smile. "With a skill like that, you are **DEFINITELY** a superhero. You should see what some of the so-called **SUPERHEROES** here call a 'special power'."

"What are you doing at Hero Con?" asks Inker.

Hiro says:

☐ I'm trying to find Doc Maybe.

☐ I'm hoping to join a superhero team.

☐ I'm planning to blow bubbles all evening.

☐ All of the above.

"You've come to the right people," says Inker. "We can help you with **ALL** of those."

"What's your name?" asks Penciller.

"Hiro," says Hiro.

"Just Hero?"

"Yes, Hiro."

"Hero or Yes-hero?" Penciller looks very confused.

"My name is just Hiro. I don't have a hero name yet." Hiro thinks for a moment. "I was thinking of calling myself **UNBURSTA BOY**."

"Well, Just-Hero, I'm afraid it doesn't work that way," says Penciller. "You don't get to **PICK** your own name; it's done by a vote."

"You don't really think I picked my **OWN** name, do you?" says Poopy Lad.

Everyone makes a suggestion, and Penciller writes them all down.

Which one would you vote for?

HIRO'S HERO NAME:

☐ BIG BUBBLES

☐ SUPER SOAPER

☐ POPSTER

☐ BUBBLE TROUBLE

☐ UNBURSTA BOY

☐ POOPY LAD JNR.

Turn the page to find out which one won! This is **VERY** exciting, isn't it.

And the winner is:

BIG BUBBLES!

Hiro looks very embarrassed. "Seriously? Big Bubbles?"

"It 100% suits you," says Inker.

Now they just need a **COOL** name for their team.

"How about The Team?" asks Inker.

"That's been done," says Penciller. "So has the A-Team. **AND THE B-TEAM**."

Hiro thinks for a moment. "What about the NEW B-TEAM?"

The others all think this is a GREAT IDEA. Who wouldn't?

"All we need now is a team **LOGO!**"

DRAW
THE LOGO

67

NEW B-TEAM ASSEMBLE!

"Can I join too?" asks a voice.
It's **UNDRAWN JOHN!** Of course he can!

DRAW
UNDRAWN
JOHN

PENCILLER   **BIG BUBBLES**   **INKER**   **UNDRAWN JOHN**

"OK," says Hiro, "we need a plan. How are we going to find Doc Maybe?"

"I have a plan," says Penciller. He pulls out a piece of paper and scribbles down a plan. "We are **HERE**, and Doc Maybe is somewhere over **HERE**. We just need to draw a line between **US** and **DOC MAYBE** and then follow it.".

Hmm, thinks Hiro, *maybe joining this team was not such a good idea.*

CHAPTER FIVE

SMILE!

"I have another idea," says Hiro. "Maybe we should go to where **SUPERVILLAINS** hang out, and see if Doc Maybe has been kidnapped and taken there."

"Whoa," says Penciller, "you're **GOOD**."

Everyone looks expectantly at Hiro.

Hiro thinks carefully. "I wonder where bad guys hang out?"

Everyone scratches their heads.

"Would this help?" asks Undrawn John, producing a copy of *Modern Villain* magazine. I know, it's bizarre. He doesn't even have pockets.

Hiro looks at the list of Heinous Hideouts.

"I suppose we should start with EJ's Office Supplies and work our way down the list," he says.

"How shall we get there?" asks Inker.

What did you expect? They've only just formed their team, so they haven't gotten their Super Team Supersonic Jet licence yet. Or bought a jet. Or even signed up for a Hero Team Van Hire Plan, for that matter.

But it looks like they are not going anywhere until someone draws the bus driver. Do you want to help?

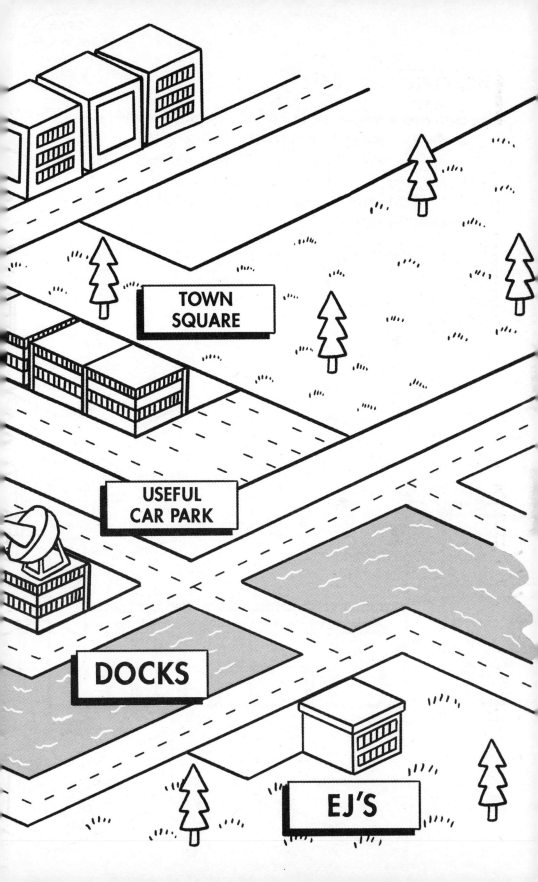

TOWN SQUARE

USEFUL CAR PARK

DOCKS

EJ'S

The bus takes **FOR EVER**. You really should have drawn a faster driver.

They finally arrive at EJ's Office Supplies. It looks like a normal, everyday store.

"**TOO** normal," says Hiro. "Let's hide behind something and stake it out."

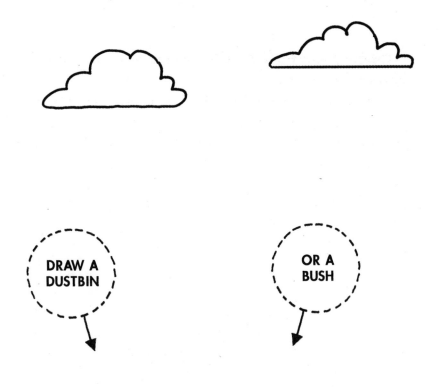

DRAW A
DUSTBIN

OR A
BUSH

Unfortunately they have all hidden
just beneath this
SECURITY CAMERA.

UH-OH! They have been spotted.
"Someone is coming," says Penciller.

Out from EJ's Office Supplies comes a very annoyed-looking supervillain.

"I've told you pesky kids already," he shouts. "No hanging around here. I'm **SERIOUS!**"

Before Hiro can say anything, Inker leaps up and charges forward.

SPLAT!

She splats The Smiler in the face with ink! Quick! Help her by drawing ink splats.

Well done, Inker! And well done, **YOU!**
The Smiler can't see. Because of the **INK** he can't
BLINK, or **WINK!**
The Smiler trips and tumbles to the ground.
"Aaargh!" he says.
And "Ooof!"
"Quick," says Hiro, "tie him up!"

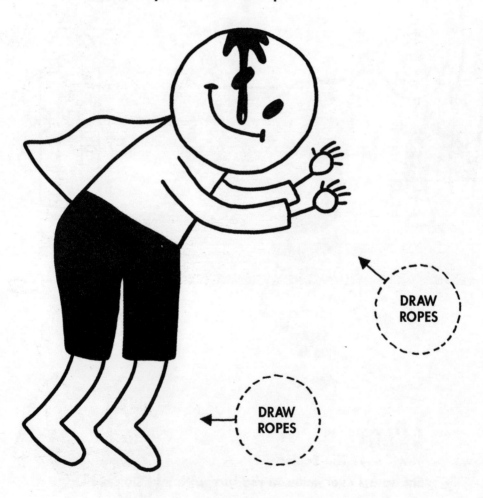

Hiro takes The Smiler's mask, gives it a quick wipe to clean off the ink, and puts it on.

"Come on. Let's see if we can use this to get into EJ's Office Supplies."

"Hey!" says The Smiler.

"What have I ever done to you guys?"

CHAPTER SIX

EVIL!

Hiro and the New B-Team approach the front door of EJ's Office Supplies.
Nervously they enter, with Hiro leading the way.

Inside it's **AWFUL!** The walls are painted magnolia.
There is terrible muzak playing over hidden speakers.
The carpet is a disgusting mix of colours.
  Hiro and his friends have never been so horrified!
  "Urgh!" says Inker, feeling unwell.

WELCOME TO EJ'S OFFICE SUPPLIES

COLOUR
THE
CARPET

"Well?" asks The Receptionist, a particularly dangerous sort of supervillain. One wrong word and you are in **TROUBLE!**

"Um," says Hiro/Smiler nervously, "I found these new recruits outside. They say they want to join us."

The Receptionist grumbles and mutters something rude under her breath.

WRITE SOMETHING RUDE*

*Wait! No, don't do that. You might get into trouble!

82

"Well, they had better sign in, then," she finally says, handing over a sign-in sheet and pencil.

VISITORS MUST SIGN IN.

_____

INKER
_____

PENCILLER
_____

UNDRAWN JOHN
_____

_____

_____

_____

The Receptionist looks over the top of her glasses at the list.

"Those names don't look like supervillain names," she says with a sneer.

Maybe you should write "EVIL" in front of each one. What do you think? That might work better.

Eventually The Receptionist lets them through to the **BACK ROOM**. Inside they find a bunch of supervillains sitting around, drinking tea, playing pool and other **SUPER EVIL** stuff like that.

DRAW A POOL CUE

DRAW A BASEBALL BAT

Hiro mutters quietly to the others, "OK, let's see if we can find out if they know anything about Doc Maybe's disappearance."

"Hey! " shouts Penciller, "Did any of you kidnap Doc Maybe?"

Oh dear...

Even Undrawn John is embarrassed, although it's hard to tell right now. Try drawing him with a big red face.

A loud alarm sounds. It's the RECRUITER TROUBLESHOOTER HOOTER.

A voice blares out of the loudspeakers, "Intruder alert! Intruder alert! Non-truthful recruits! Beware! Good guys in disguise!"

A trap snaps shut on Hiro and the New B-Team.

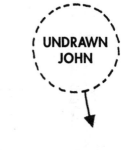
UNDRAWN
JOHN

FOLD THE PAGE OVER

It's a...

FOLDED PAGE HOLDING CAGE!

"Well, well," says Unpleasant Desmond, "who do we have here? Some no-good do-gooders."

"I think Evil Jeff will be very interested in meeting you."

Oh no! Not **EVIL JEFF**, Doodletown's greatest supervillain. The criminal responsible for the Great Crayon Meltdown and the infamous Paper Clip Entanglement.

The New B-Team are in **SO** much trouble!

The villains escort Hiro and his friends to meet...

EVIL JEFF!

The New B-Team stand nervously in front of Evil Jeff as he glowers down at them.

"You pathetic superheroes," says Evil Jeff. "You think you can come in here to my secret hideout and thwart my evil plan to **DESTROY** all of Doodletown's drawing material, thereby allowing me to control the whole town with my hoarded stash of paper?"

"Um, no," says Hiro, "we were just wondering where Doc Maybe was."

"You mean you are not here to foil my plan to burn all the colouring books and sketchbooks in Doodletown?" asks Evil Jeff.

Hiro, Penciller and Inker shake their heads. Undrawn John probably does too, but it's hard to tell.

"Oh, OK," says Evil Jeff, getting flustered. "Forget I said anything. Let's pretend this never happened."

"Shall we lock them up, boss?" asks Unpleasant Desmond.

Evil Jeff looks distracted. "Yes. Yes, of course. We can't let anyone know about my evil plan to also corner the market in sparkle glue and sticky tape."

What a **CRAFTY FIEND!** Is there no end to Evil Jeff's dastardly plans?

CHAPTER SEVEN

ESCAPE!

Hiro and his friends are escorted into Evil Jeff's Eleven Level Elevator. Unpleasant Desmond presses the button for Prison Cells, which is way, way down in the sub-sub-basement of Evil Jeff's lair.

(Hey! How about pressing **ALL** the buttons to annoy him!)

●	0 Reception
●	-1 Canteen and Games Room
●	-2 Throne Room
●	-3 Evil Plan Planning Room
●	-4 Map Room
●	-5 Kaiju Zoo

●	-6 Meeting Room
●	-7 Toilets
●	-8 Evil Jeff's Bedroom KEEP OUT!
●	-9 Evil Vehicle Garage
●	-10 Evil Plan Equipment Store
●	-11 Prison Cells

Eventually, the lift reaches the sub-sub-basement. Unpleasant Desmond pushes our heroes into a cell and slams the door behind them. There seems to be no way out.

"Evil Jeff's plan sounds **DESPICABLE**," says Inker. "The odds are against us, but we've got to break out, go up there and do something about it!"

"Or we could just **ESCAPE** and run away. And maybe tell some **REAL SUPERHEROES**," says Penciller, looking very nervous.

What do you think they should do?

Do you think they should break out and foil Evil Jeff's plan? Then turn to page 94.

Or should they just try to run away and warn everyone? Turn to page 102.

"We need to spoil Evil Jeff's plan," says Hiro. "Any ideas, anyone?"

"I can't see any way out," says Penciller, "Apart from that vent up there. If only there was a way to get up there."

Everyone looks at him. Everyone looks at the vent over their heads.

"Well," says Hiro slowly, "you are a giant pencil. You could Create Your Own ladder for us to climb up."

Penciller looks at them all. "Yes," he says, his eyes widening. "Yes, I suppose I could."

Help Penciller draw a ladder for them to climb.

After climbing the ladder that Penciller and you drew,
Hiro and his team crawl through the ventilation ducts.

Hiro comes to another vent and looks down.

"I can see the stuff Evil Jeff plans to use to
DESTROY all the paper," he whispers.

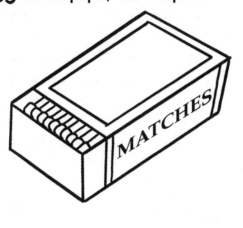

ADD
TWIGS AND
STICKS

DRAW
MORE
LOGS

Suddenly, the duct breaks! It can't support all their weight. Undrawn John shouldn't have eaten all those undrawn pies!

They all tumble towards the floor.

With quick thinking, Hiro fires bubbles at his friends, to protect them.

Quick! Draw bubbles around everyone!

Phew! They land safely. No one is injured, thanks to Hiro's quick thinking and your quick drawing.

Hiro and the New B-Team explore the storeroom.

"We've got to make all these matches unusable," says Hiro. "We've got to make them **WET**."

Have you any ideas? How about going back and popping the bubbles you just drew by poking holes in the page with your pencil?

BRILLIANT! The moisture from the bubbles on the opposite page soaks the matches. They'll never start a fire now.

"Look what I've found," says Inker. "It's Evil Jeff's plan!
I'll change it with some ink."
Scribble out all the letters that Inker has underlined.

THE EVIL JEFF PLAN

TO PRACTICE LOOKING EVIL
ESPECIALLY AS I AIM TO
ACHIEVE SUPER-VILLAINY
AS THE GREATEST BADDY
IN THE LAND
BY COMBUSTING
ALL DRAWING BOOKS
AND ART SUPPLIES!

HOORAY!

Undrawn John studies the big pile of logs.

"I guess I could undraw all this bonfire wood with my **INVISIBLE PENCIL!**"

Have you ever seen an Invisible Pencil?

No? Me neither.

"It's not very good for drawing," he says, "but it's great for **UNDRAWING**."

The New B-Team watch in awe as Undrawn John draws a shape around the logs, and they all **DISAPPEAR**."

Tear out this piece of page to make the logs disappear.

Look! There is an escape route hidden behind the logs. It leads directly to the fire escape stairs.

Hiro and the team all climb through.

"Let's get out of here!" says Penciller, a little too enthusiastically.

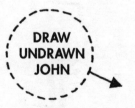

DRAW
UNDRAWN
JOHN

Penciller leads the team as they ~~make their~~ ~~ESCAPE to the outside~~, I mean, race upstairs to FOIL Evil Jeff's plan.

SECRET
FIRE
ESCAPE
STAIRS

Turn to page 112 to continue.

"I agree," says Hiro. "We should escape and warn the mayor of Evil Jeff's plan."

"There is a 1 in 787 chance of escaping a prison. How are WE going to get out of here?" asks Inker.

They bang the walls. They are solid.

They stamp on the floor. No trapdoors.

They try the door handle. No luck.

There is a knock on the door.

KNOCK KNOCK

"Hello," says a voice. "It's Undrawn John! They forgot to put me in the cell because they didn't realize I was here."

Having the **UNDRAWN** superpower clearly has its advantages!

"Great!" says Hiro. "Can you open the door from the outside?"

"Yes, there is a spare undrawn key hanging outside."

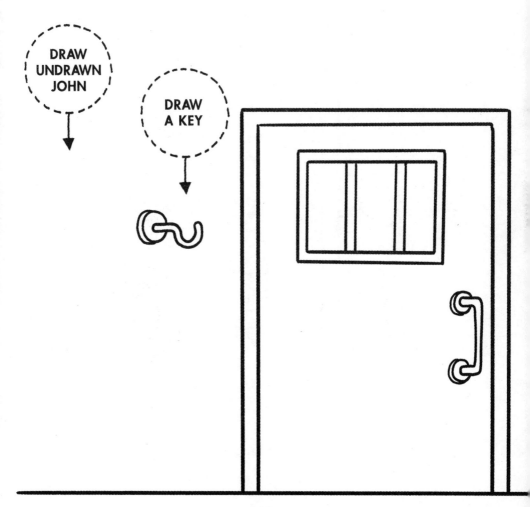

Undrawn John opens the door and releases the New B-Team.

Inker gives Undrawn John a big hug. "I LOVE your superpower, UJ. It's 120% better than everyone else's," she says.

Undrawn John blushes (probably).

They run to the elevator. At this level there are only two buttons. Which should they press?

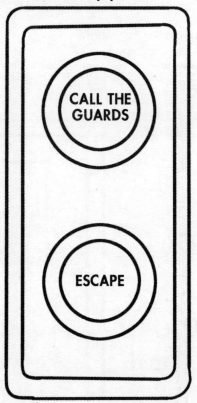

If you pressed the top button, then turn to page 132.

If you pressed the bottom button then turn to page 137.

They scramble into the elevator and press the button for the reception. Now all they have to do is sneak past The Receptionist.

The elevator rises slowly up through Evil Jeff's secret base.

Suddenly there is a **CRUNCH!**

Followed by a **SPTANG!**

The elevator grinds to a halt.

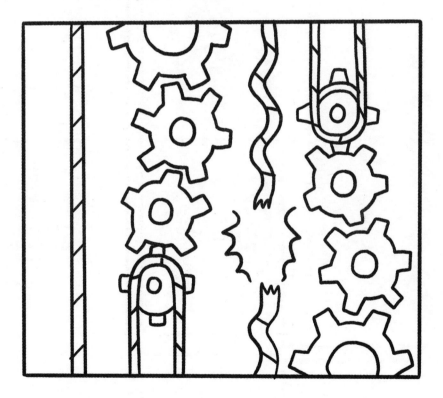

Oh dear!

How are they going to get out of this one?

"Lift me up to that access hatch," says Hiro.

Sure enough, the hatch lifts easily. With the help of his friends, Hiro squeezes through.

"I can see light at the top," he calls out.

Everyone climbs out on to the roof.

"How are we going to get up there?" asks Penciller.

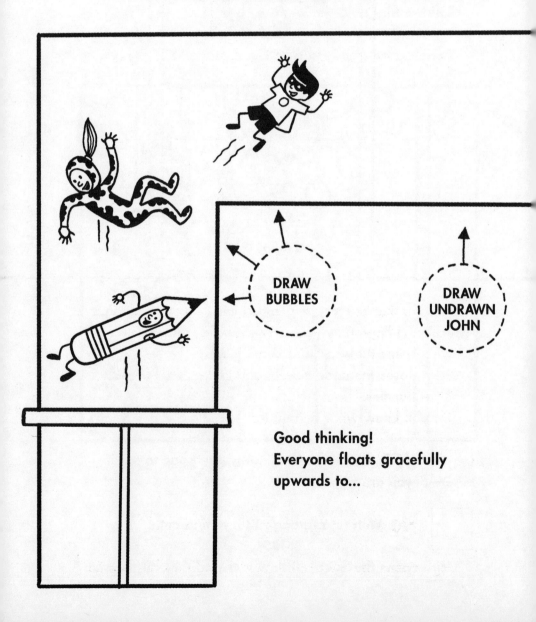

DRAW
BUBBLES

DRAW
UNDRAWN
JOHN

Good thinking!
Everyone floats gracefully
upwards to...

... level 5.

Hiro forces the doors apart, and they all squeeze through.

They find themselves in a short corridor with one other door.

"Ooh, is that like a petting zoo? I love petting zoos," says Penciller. "I hope they have some bunnies and a donkey."

Hiro opens the door and peers inside.

Hiro closes the door quietly and looks at his friends.

"Not bunnies," he says.

Do you know what a kaiju is?

YES. OK, Know-It-All, turn the page to see if you are right.

NO. Well turn to page 138, to find out!

Hiro opens the door a little wider and they all peep in.

OMG! ITS A GIGANTIC MONSTER!
HAVING A SANDWICH!
It's feeding time in the Kaiju Zoo, and kaijus love
chicken sandwiches. UNCOOKED chicken sandwiches!

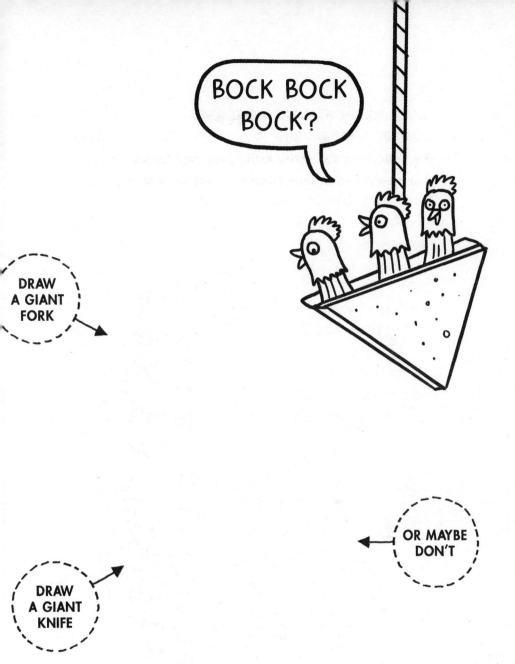

"This is worse than we thought," says Hiro. "We can't leave. We've got to put a stop to Evil Jeff's plans."
"OK," says Hiro, "here's what we have to do."

"Rescue the chickens?" suggests Penciller.

"Well, yes, that," says Hiro, "but we've got to distract the kaiju first. OK, Undrawn John, you have to creep in there unseen and make loads of noise to distract the kaiju. Then, Inker, I need you to sneak in and draw a big black circle that looks like a hole in the ground between the monster and the chickens. The kaiju will think it's a pit and hopefully back away. Next, I need you, Penciller, to go around the back and draw a net to catch the chickens when I release them. I'll float up on a bubble and set the chickens free when the kaiju's not looking and drop them into the net."

Everyone nods. Except Undrawn John. Who knows if he's nodding or not?

"What do you think, Inker? Can you give me a number crunch?" asks Hiro.

HOW MUCH WE WANT TO SURVIVE: 100%

CHANCE OF CHICKENS SURVIVING IF WE DO NOTHING: 0%

CHANCE OF KAIJU STOMPING ALL OVER US AND EATING US FOR DESSERT: 66.666%

CHANCE OF ACTUALLY SURVIVING:

Can you work it out?* Show your workings.

*Hint: it's 33.333%

CHAPTER EIGHT

SHOWDOWN!

Suddenly a voice yells, "They've escaped!"

It's Evil Jeff and his cronies, coming down the stairs.

Evil Jeff stops on the second last step (to make himself look taller) and points at the New B-Team. "Get th—"

But before he can finish his sentence, there is a loud yell:

"UNDRAAAAAAWN JOHN!"

LOOK! It's Undrawn John charging like a crazy orangutan towards Evil Jeff!

"What th—" says Evil Jeff, totally confused.

He's confused because you haven't drawn Crazy Undrawn Orangutan John yet!

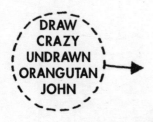

DRAW
CRAZY
UNDRAWN
ORANGUTAN
JOHN

"Did he just—?" asks Inker.

"Yup," says Hiro, with a sigh. "I suppose we'd better help."

The New B-Team charge at Evil Jeff's crew.

"CHARGE!" says Hiro.

"YAHOOOOO!" says Inker.

"OOO-ER!" says Penciller.

"THE HUH?!" says Evil Jeff.

"YIKES!" says Unpleasant Desmond.

"MUMMY!" says Mucky Savage.

"OOF!" says Disaster Joan, as Undrawn John clatters into her and knocks her over.

"At least I got a chicken,"
says Undrawn John.

Hiro battles his way through the crowd, and finally confronts Evil Jeff.

Hiro is about to blast him with bubbles when Evil Jeff shouts, "Wait, Hiro! I am your FATHER!"

"No you're not," says Hiro.

"It was worth a try," says Evil Jeff, as he lunges for a lever on the wall.

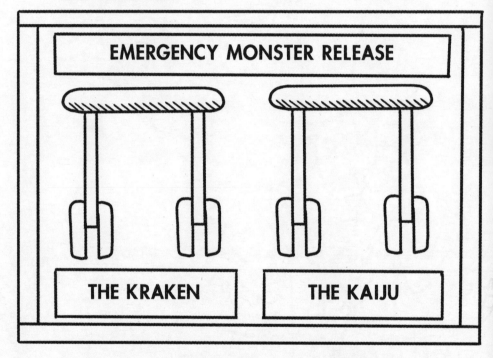

EMERGENCY MONSTER RELEASE

THE KRAKEN

THE KAIJU

"RELEASE THE KRAKEN!" he yells, and pulls the lever on the left. Nothing happens.

"Oh, I forgot, the Kraken is hibernating," Evil Jeff mutters. "Oh well, RELEASE THE KAIJU!"

Before Hiro can stop him, he pulls the lever on the right.

With a

Evil Jeff's gigantic monster is free!
"Where's my saddle?" shouts Evil Jeff.

DRAW A
SADDLE

Draw him a saddle. He doesn't deserve it, but the
story will be over too quickly if you don't.

KERRASH!

The kaiju knocks down the wall and stomps out into the street.

Cars **HONK!** People **SCREAM!** Birds **POOP!** **OH NO!** The kaiju is about to stomp on a police van!

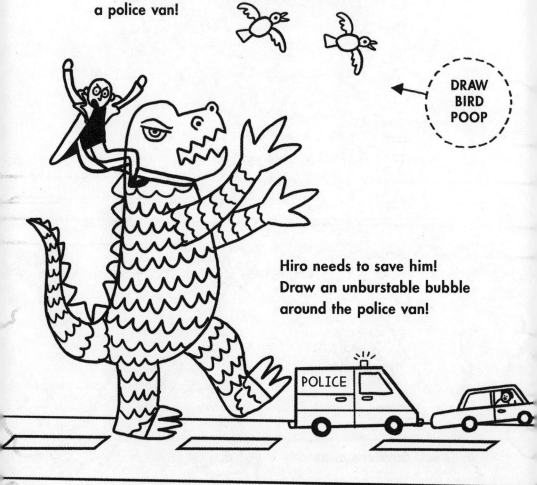

DRAW BIRD POOP

Hiro needs to save him! Draw an unburstable bubble around the police van!

POLICE

"Woo-hoo!" shouts Evil Jeff. "I should have just done this in the first place instead of making those other **CRAZY** plans!"

The kaiju bellows, and takes a chomp out of the motorway bridge.

Quick! Save the cars!

DRAW BUBBLE TO SAVE THE CAR

Evil Jeff rides the Kaiju towards City Hall. The mayor squeals.

"Say a prayer, Mayor Squarehair," yells Evil Jeff with glee. "Your chances of re-election are about to be squashed!"

"We must pass a law to stop you," squeals the mayor.

Quick! Do you think you can draft up a city regulation making the stomping of mayors by monsters illegal, and get the city council to vote and pass it before the Kaiju stomps on the mayor?

☐ **YES**, turn to page 140.

☐ **NO**. OK, on to the next page!

This is it! Hiro has to save the day! He's got to make the **BIGGEST** bubble ever! A bubble so big, and **SO** strong that it will contain a gigantic, rampaging monster! And he can't do it without **YOUR** help!

Do you think you can draw a bubble around the **ENTIRE** kaiju?

Well, don't just sit there! **DO IT!**

Hiro carefully aims his Bubble Blaster and squeezes the trigger. A bubble forms, grows bigger and bigger, and envelops the monster.

YoU DID IT!

The kaiju roars! It scratches and bites the bubble, but it won't burst.

DRAW IT AGAIN →

There it goes, drifting away on a gentle breeze.

"Darn it," says Evil Jeff, "I give up!"

Suddenly, there is a whoosh of rockets. An armoured superhero drops from the sky, and lands beside Hiro. It's DOC MAYBE as NORI MAN!

"I heard there was a monster on the loose. I'm here to save the day!" he says.

He strikes a heroic pose and looks around.

"Where is it?" he asks.

Hiro and Evil Jeff point to the sky.

"Oh," says Doc Maybe.

CHAPTER NINE

INVOICE!

A crowd gathers around and cheers. They lift Doc Maybe up on their shoulders and carry him up the steps of Town Hall.

Hiro and the New B-Team all look at each other.

"What just happened there?" asks Inker.

"I think," says Hiro, "we've been out-foxed by the Doc. He's going to take all the credit."

WRITE THIS SIGN

DEFINITELY MAYBE!

DOC ROCKS!

Doc Maybe stands on the podium beside Mayor Squarehair, who claps his hands together excitedly.

"Doodletown extends its thanks to you, Doctor Maybe," the mayor says. "Once again you have saved the day!"

Everybody claps and cheers. Doc Maybe waves and says modestly, "Oh, it was really nothing."

"You're right!" shouts a voice from the back of the crowd. "You did nothing." It's Inker, and she is furious. "Hiro is the real hero," she continues, pointing at Hiro, who suddenly feels **VERY** embarrassed. Look! His face has gone bright red.

COLOUR HIS FACE

"Well, of course," says Doc Maybe, "I couldn't have done it without Hiro."

He waves to Hiro and calls him up to the top of the steps. Hiro reluctantly climbs up, while the crowd claps politely.

"Take a bow, Hiro," mutters Doc Maybe. "You did very well, considering I wasn't here to help."

"So you are responsible for stopping Evil Jeff and his monster?" the mayor asks.

"I suppose so," says Hiro. "Along with my friends, of course."

"Well, I'm glad you are taking responsibility," he says. "There has been a lot of damage, and someone has to pay for it."

He holds out a piece of paper. "Sign here, please."

Office of the Mayor
Doodletown

INVOICE

Destruction of motorway bridge:	$800,000
Replacement police cars:	$60,000
Repair of gigantic potholes:	$32,000
Ruining the mayor's hair:	$68

TOTAL: $892,068

Please sign your name here _____

Gosh, that sure is a lot of money! I hope you didn't sign that invoice. There is no way Hiro can afford that.

WHAT? You signed it?

☐ **YES**. What were you thinking? Go back and use your Nullification Device (eraser) to rub out your name immediately!

☐ **NO**, of course I didn't. I'm not daft.

Doc Maybe pats Hiro on the shoulder.
"Now you know why I'm a billionaire," he says. "With **GREAT POWER** comes **GREAT LIABILITY**."

"In fact, Hiro," he continues, "I'm thinking of retiring. I've had enough of being superheroes. I want to be a Doctor of Medicine, not just a Doctor of Inventions."

Hiro is shocked.

Mayor Squarehair is shocked.

Inker and Penciller are shocked.

Even Undrawn John is shocked. Although you'd never know.

DRAW
UNDRAWN
JOHN*

* Looking shocked, of course

Doc Maybe continues, "The truth is, Hiro, this has all been a test. I wanted to see how a new hero would cope if I wasn't around. And you did pretty well. I knew when you won the Doodletown Doodling Contest* that you had the imagination and creativity to take over. I just needed to find out if you had the COURAGE."

He holds out the famous Maybe Knot, the source of his power. It pulses and glows with mysterious light.

"Here," he says. "It's yours if you want it."

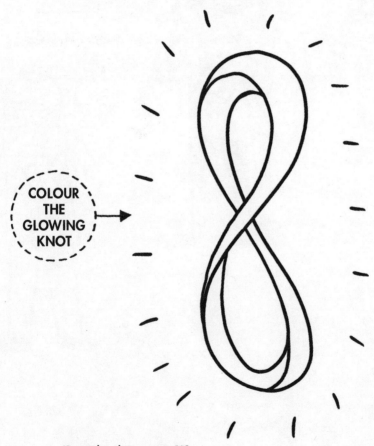

COLOUR
THE
GLOWING
KNOT

*Remember that on page 16?

Hiro stares at it. What is Hiro to do? What would **you** do?

TAKE THE JOB

Turn to page 142

**NO, THANKS!
I'LL PASS**

Turn to page 139

OUT OF ORDER

Well, lucky for you, the "CALL THE GUARDS" button is out of order.

Back to page 105.

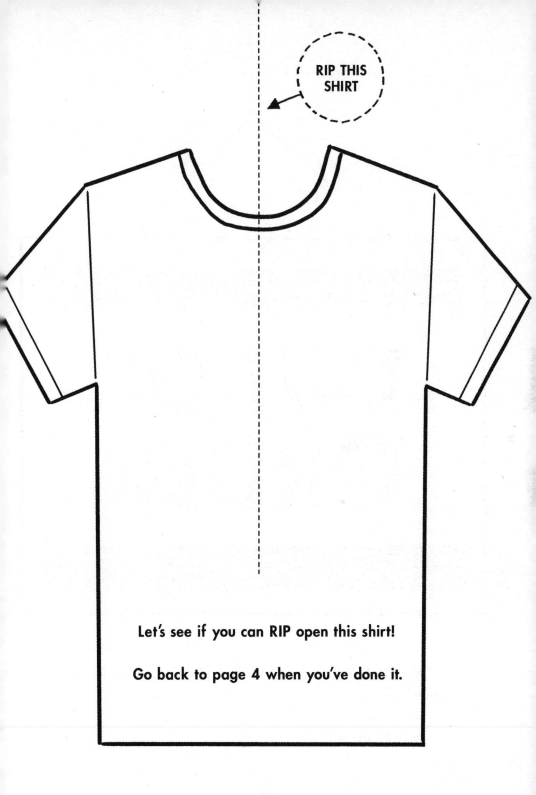

RIP THIS
SHIRT

Let's see if you can RIP open this shirt!

Go back to page 4 when you've done it.

That was my good shirt!

HERO CON
DOODLETOWN'S
NO. 1 SUPERHERO CONVENTION

Location:
DOODLETOWN HALL

Time:
2.00 p.m.

Special Guest Star
DOC MAYBE

COSPLAY PRIZES

Featuring:
MOUSE MASTER
MINI-HEAD
SOCK-EATER LAD
JOIN-THE-DOTS DOTTY

THE END

Sorry! Hope we didn't frighten you too much!

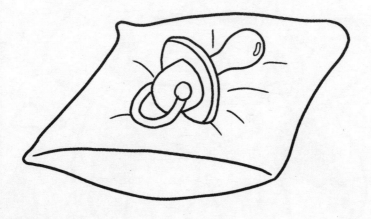

Only joking! Back to page 8.

WELL DONE!

TEN OUT OF TEN

FOR INGENUITY!

Now, back to page 105.

WICKEDPEDIA
The Encyclopaedia for Bad Guys

Kaiju
Kaijū (怪獣 **kaijū?**)
(from Japanese "strange beast")

Kaiju are enormous Japanese
monsters that stomp around
and smash up cities.
See *Godzilla*.

Kraken
Kraken (/ˈkraːkən/)

The Kraken is a gigantic sea
monster that looks like a huge
squid. Avoid at all costs.
Not to be confused with Kaiju.

Back to page 108!

"No, thanks," says Hiro. "I'd prefer not to be a superhero, if you don't mind. I'd prefer to be something useful, like an illustrator."

"Oh," says Doc Maybe. "I know that feeling. Well, best of luck."

THE END

"What about you?" says Doc Maybe to Undrawn John. But that's another story.*

*See page 141.

CITY ORDINANCE NO. 359

Under the Code for Behaviour of Supervillains, the city of Doodletown hereby makes it unlawful for large monsters to stomp on city officials.

Violations are subject to a fine of $1,000 per stomping incident, and/or 23 hours of community service.

Signed

_____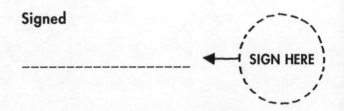

Witnessed by
DAVID "DOC" MAYBE

Hooray! You did it! You defeated Evil Jeff by regulatory means. Now go to page 124.

FINISH
UNDRAWN
JOHN

UNDRAWN
JOHN RETURNS

BY
YOU

"OK," says Hiro. "I'll DO IT! As long as I get to change my name to KNOT BIG BUBBLES."

The crowd cheers and lifts Hiro up on their shoulders! Hooray for SUPER HIRO!

COLOUR THE FIREWORKS

THE END

CREATE YOUR OWN

SPY MISSION

Turn the page for a sample chapter!

CHAPTER ONE
MISSION!

If you were on a plane and needed to get off quickly would you do this?

YES, obviously, if you were **ETHAN DOODLE**, Super Spy!

Welcome to the world of Ethan Doodle.

No **THRILL** is too thrilling!

No **DANGER** is too dangerous!

No **PARACHUTE** is . . . bad.

"**AAAAAARGH!** I forgot to pack one!" says Ethan.

This is going to be a very short book unless you can help him out. You had better draw a parachute to save him or he will need to change his name to Ethan Doodle, Super Splat!

Phew! OK, so where were we?

Oh, yes: Ethan. Falling.

This is a very exciting start, isn't it? I bet you are wondering **WHAT** is going on.

Well, I can tell you this. . . See that train at the bottom of the page? Ethan needs to get on board it as quickly as possible before it goes into the tunnel on the opposite page.

Ethan lands on the roof of the train and grabs on tightly. Ahead of him he sees the train about to go into the tunnel. If he doesn't do something quickly he's going to be splattered like a bug on a windscreen.

Ethan runs along the roof and then **LEAPS** off. He grabs on to the side and swings through an **OPEN** window.

Oops! I forgot to mention you need to **DRAW** an open window for him to swing through. Quick!

Ethan gets on board the train. He needs to get to the other end of the train as quickly as possible. It's an **EMERGENCY**! He runs through the carriage. He leaps over a big suitcase in the aisle.

He crawls along the luggage rack to avoid a crying baby.

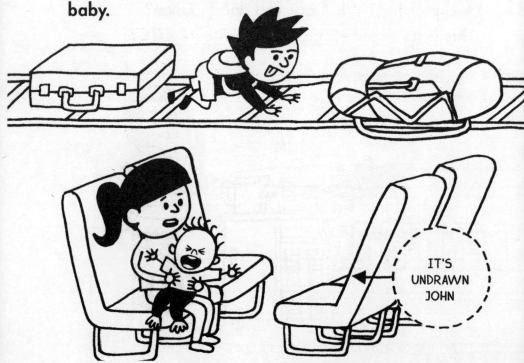

IT'S
UNDRAWN
JOHN

He crawls under a seat because, well, it's more exciting than just running down the aisle.

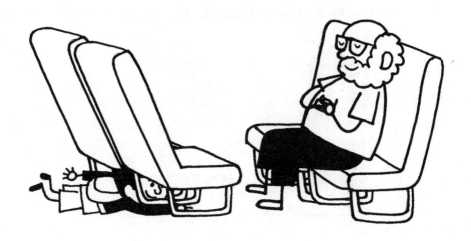

He stops to get a cup of tea from the snack trolley.
A cup of tea? What are you doing, Ethan?
This is no time for tea. It's an **EMERGENCY!**

Ethan finally reaches the **TOILET** at the other end of the train.

Yes, it's **THAT** kind of emergency.

But it looks like the toilet is occupied. Oh no, this is a disaster! Unless. . .

Quick! Change the sign to **UNOCCUPIED** while no one is looking.

Well done! Emergency averted! You saved the day.

"Phew," says Ethan. "That was close. Another ten seconds and I would have ▬▬▬ my ▬▬▬."

Yes, well, thank you very much for that information, Ethan. I'm sure we all needed to know that. Thank goodness this is a book about **SPIES** because that will hopefully be **BLANKED OUT** before it is printed.

Ethan looks around the cubicle. "Um, there's no toilet paper. . ."

Just when you thought this book could not get any more exciting.